For Mia—
wash your hands

SIMON & SCHUSTER BOOKS FOR YOUNG READERS
An imprint of Simon & Schuster Children's Publishing Division
1230 Avenue of the Americas, New York, New York 10020
SIMON & SCHUSTER BOOKS FOR YOUNG READERS is a trademark of Simon & Schuster, Inc.
For information about special discounts for bulk purchases, please contact Simon & Schuster
Special Sales at 1-866-506-1949 or business@simonandschuster.com.
The Simon & Schuster Speakers Bureau can bring authors to your live event. For more
information or to book an event, contact the Simon & Schuster Speakers Bureau at
1-866-248-3049 or visit our website at www.simonspeakers.com.
Book design by Lizzy Bromley
The text for this book is set in Schnitzle.
The illustrations for this book are rendered in Photoshop.
Manufactured in China
1014 SCP
2 4 6 8 10 9 7 5 3 1
Library of Congress Cataloging-in-Publication Data
Krall, Dan, author, illustrator.
Sick Simon / by Dan Krall. — First edition.
pages cm
Summary: By not covering his mouth or washing his hands, Simon spreads his cold to his
teacher and classmates, much to the delight of three germs named Virus, Protozoa, and Bacteria.
ISBN 978-1-4424-9097-0 (hardcover : alk. paper)
ISBN 978-1-4424-9098-7 (eBook)
[1. Cold (Disease)—Fiction. 2. Sick—Fiction.] I. Title.
PZ7.K85865Si 2014
[E]—dc23   2013041862

SICK SIMON

by Dan Krall

Simon & Schuster Books for Young Readers
New York London Toronto Sydney New Delhi

It was Monday! Simon didn't care if he had a cold.
He was ready for the best week ever!

He kissed his family good morning and

had his favorite breakfast.

He rode the bus to school and had fun the whole way.

School was Simon's favorite place.

Math was Simon's best subject,
so he was sure to participate A LOT.

On Tuesday, Simon got to take care of Mr. Warbles, the class chinchilla.

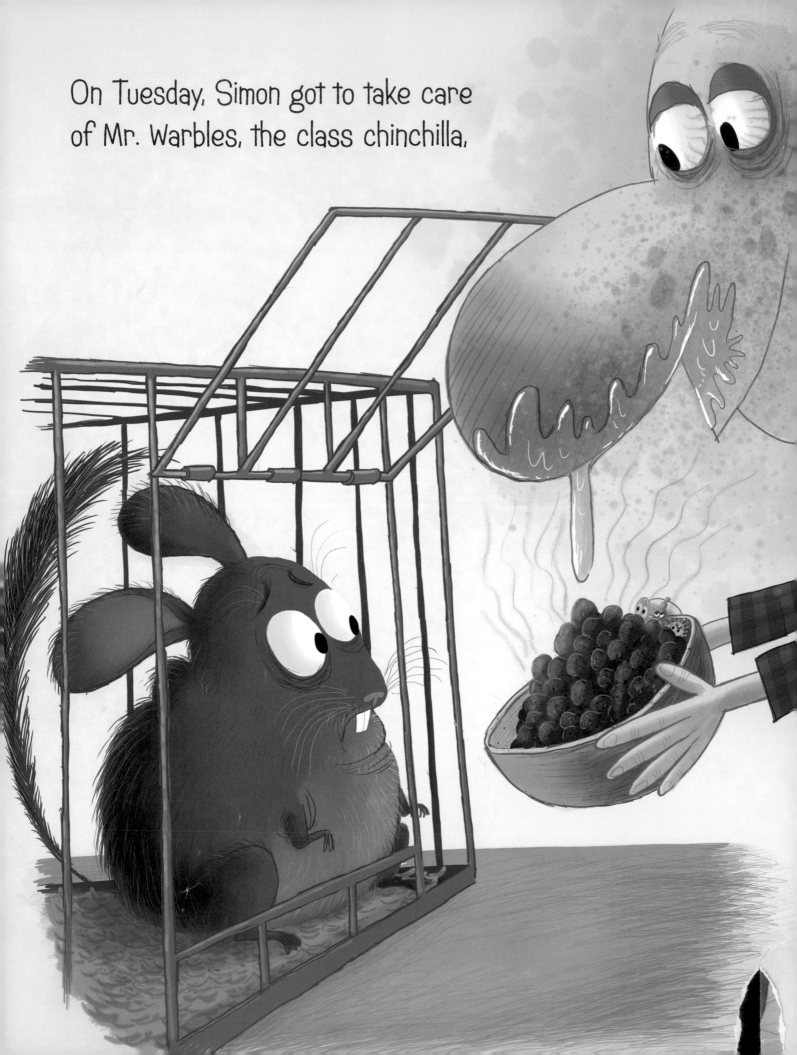

share snacks with friends,

and have show-and-tell.

Wednesday's field trip was a treat.

Although recess on
Thursday was a blast,

what Simon was really
looking forward to . . .

was Friday's superbig game of kickball.

On the way home, Simon started thinking maybe this wasn't the best week after all.

Hey, Simon, nice work this week. You're the man!!
What? Who are you guys?

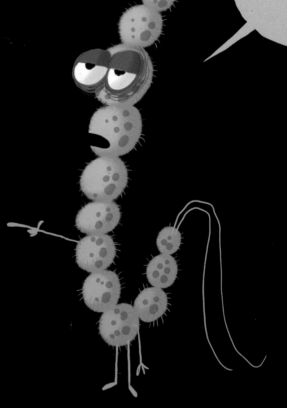

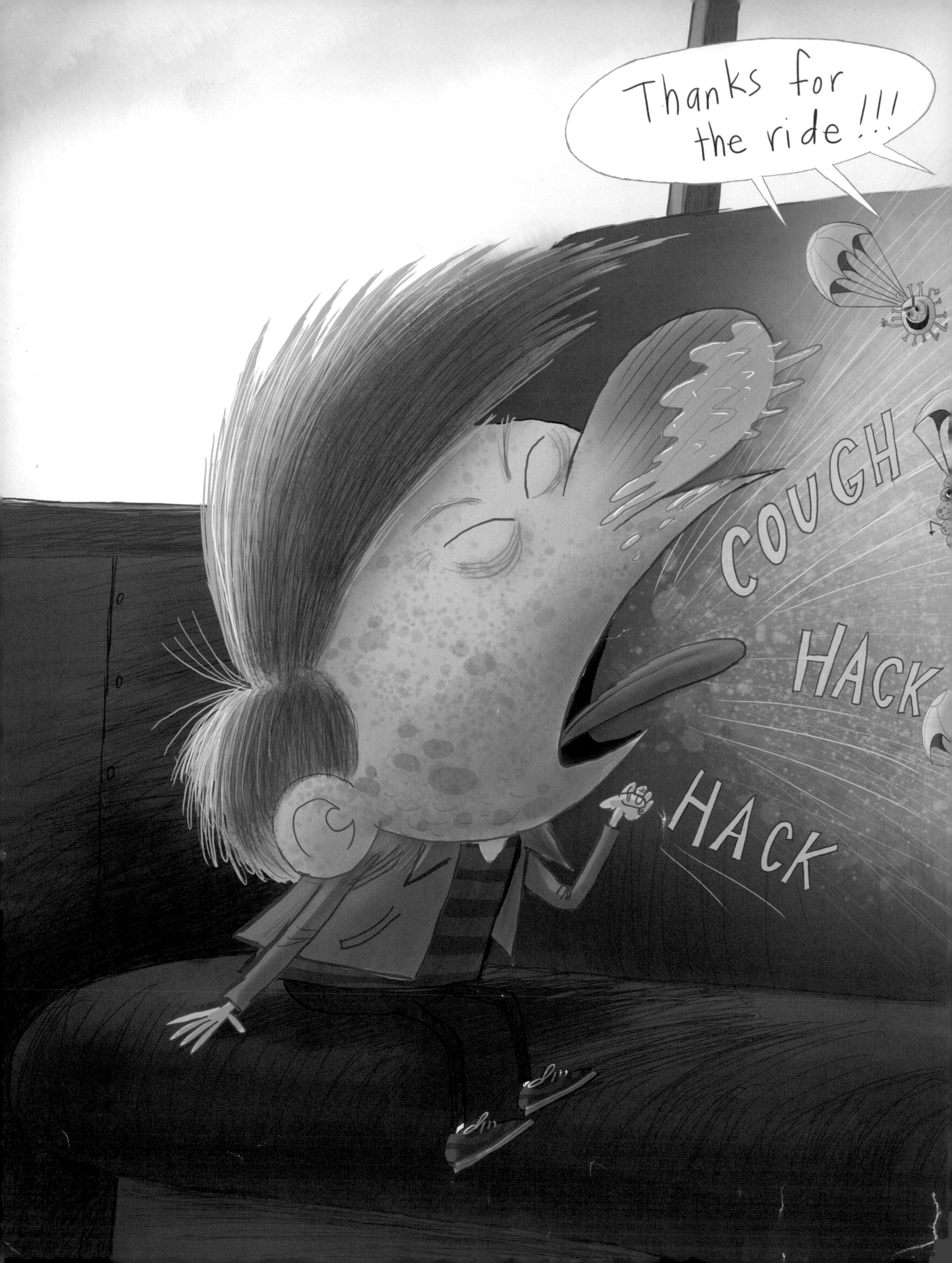
Thanks for the ride!!!
COUGH
HACK
HACK

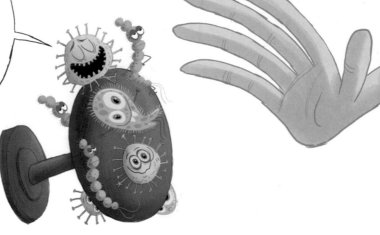

And that's how the magic happens!

You never wash your hands!

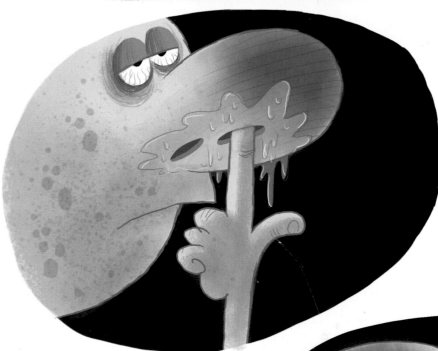

You never cover your mouth!

You sneeze on EVERYTHING!!

You LOVE spreading germs!!

With that, Simon raced off the bus and did
something the germs did not like one bit.

Simon covered his mouth when he sneezed,
and coughed and blew his nose with a tissue,

then he threw the tissue into the trash can.

Then he went to the sink and washed
his hands with warm soapy water,

which sent the germs packing.

Simon rested all weekend.

By Monday, Simon woke up feeling as good as new. . . .

He was ready to go back to his favorite place
in the whole world and . . .

to have the best week ever!